Tooth or Dare

READ ALL THE SHARK SCHOOL BOOKS!

SHARK SCHOOL

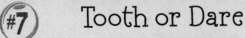

#7 Tooth or Dare

BY DAVY OCEAN
ILLUSTRATED BY AARON BLECHA

ALADDIN   New York   London   Toronto   Sydney   New Delhi

WITH THANKS TO PAUL EBBS

This book is a work of fiction. Any references to historical events, real people, or real places are used fictitiously. Other names, characters, places, and events are products of the author's imagination, and any resemblance to actual events or places or persons, living or dead, is entirely coincidental.

ALADDIN

An imprint of Simon & Schuster Children's Publishing Division
1230 Avenue of the Americas, New York, NY 10020
First Aladdin paperback edition November 2016
Text copyright © 2016 by Hothouse Fiction
Illustrations copyright © 2016 by Aaron Blecha
Also available in an Aladdin hardcover edition.
All rights reserved, including the right of reproduction in whole or in part in any form.
ALADDIN is a trademark of Simon & Schuster, Inc., and related logo is a
registered trademark of Simon & Schuster, Inc.
For information about special discounts for bulk purchases, please contact
Simon & Schuster Special Sales at 1-866-506-1949 or business@simonandschuster.com.
The Simon & Schuster Speakers Bureau can bring authors to your live event. For more
information or to book an event contact the Simon & Schuster Speakers Bureau at 1-866-248-3049
or visit our website at www.simonspeakers.com.
Cover designed by Karin Paprocki
Interior designed by Mike Rosamilia
The text of this book was set in Write Demibd.
Manufactured in the United States of America 0916 OFF
2 4 6 8 10 9 7 5 3 1
Library of Congress Control Number 2016936363
ISBN 978-1-4814-6547-2 (hc)
ISBN 978-1-4814-6546-5 (pbk)
ISBN 978-1-4814-6548-9 (eBook)

CHAPTER 1

"Two hundred and nineteen . . . two hundred and twenty . . . two hundred and . . ."

Hummmmmmmmmmmmmmmmmmmmmmmmmmmmmmmmmmm!!!!!

"Arrrrrrrrrrrrrrrrrrrrrrrrrrrrrrrrrrrgh!"

Tinkle. *Crunch.*

Crrrraaaaaaaaaaaashh!!!!

As the huge pyramid of teeth I've been counting crashes to the bedroom floor, I glare at Humphrey, my humming-fish alarm clock, from *both* sides of my hammer.

The glare is meant to make him *terrified* . . . but in this case it's more *laughing-i-fied.*

Humphrey floats onto his back as bubbles of laughter explode from his gills.

With a sudden *flash*, Larry the Lantern Fish starts glowing like a ship's fog light. Larry always gets too bright when he's startled.

"Is it time to get up already?" he says sleepily, finning his eyes and dimming his light.

I float around and sigh at the teeth scattered all over the carpet.

Okay, I'd better explain.

How many teeth do you have? Count them. While you're doing that, I'll list all you need to know about *my* teeth.

Sharks have about a squillion unbelievably sharp teeth.

I have row after row of them in my mouth.

They fall out all the time and are replaced within a day.

If there was a Tooth Fairy for sharks (like you leggy air breathers have) we'd all be millionaires by the time we're eight.

But we don't have a Tooth Fairy, and they'd probably run out of money in half a day.

Instead we collect our teeth in a jar and have a competition at school to see

4

who has lost the most each year.

That's why I was counting them out on top of my bedside crabinet.

But now they're scattered all over the floor and I have to count them all out *again*! (Humphrey starting to hum made me jump and the teeth went flying.)

Humphrey obviously thinks this is the funniest thing he's ever seen. I can still hear him snickering as I start shoveling the teeth back into the jar with my tail.

The reason I woke up before my alarm-clock fish went off is because I was too excited to sleep. And the reason I was too excited to sleep is because we're nearly at the end of the school year. In *one week* the prize for who has lost the most teeth will be handed out in class by our teacher, Mrs. Shelby.

To be honest it's a junky prize: a replica of a great white's tooth stuck in a piece of driftwood. Well, the driftwood isn't a replica,  there's bunches of that around—but the shark tooth is made from carved coral.

I wouldn't mind if it was a real Great White's Tooth—that would be cool. But coral?

No.

But I *do* want to win the competition. Mainly to beat Rick Reef the reef shark. He always wins. For the past three years I've been close, but he's managed to beat me *every single time.*

This year will be different though. The last time I'd counted I'd lost two hundred and seventy-three teeth. Last year Rick only lost two hundred and seventy-one and he won the competition.

"I don't know why you're bothering," says Larry from behind me.

"Yeah, you know Rick's gonna win. He always does," says Humphrey.

I keep shoveling. They're only trying to rile me up.

"I heard Rick's lost so many teeth this year he has to suck his breakfast to death," Humphrey says, snickering.

I'm about to come back with the wittiest put down in the history of put downs . . . but I can't use it because Mom is calling upstairs, "Harry-Warry! Time for brekkie-wekkie!"

I go downstairs and once I wriggle out of Mom's finbrace (she hugs me so tight it makes my eyes bulge out of my hammerlike balloons), I dart into the kitchen. Dad is floating at the table eating his sea-cereal with one fin while checking the news on his cool new octopiPAD. He's swiping across the screen, flicking through page after page of boring news.

I've been on my best behavior all week because he promised that if I'm good, he'll let me use the octopiPAD over the weekend to play BrineCraft. I sit quietly while he flicks. Mom puts a bowl of Kelp Krispies in front of me and I bite down extra hard on them, hoping to pop out another tooth.

"Harry!" Dad says, lifting his nose from the octopiPAD and giving me his squintiest look. "Can't you eat a bit quieter? I'm trying to read the news and all I can hear is your teeth crunching like seashells in a washing machine!"

"Sorry ... *crunch* ... Dad ... *crunch* ...

I'm trying to knock . . . *crunch* . . . a . . . few . . . more . . . GWULFFFFFFFFF!!!"

Dad pops some marine-beans into my chompy mouth and pushes my jaws closed. "Just be quiet—and take a look at this."

He holds up the octopiPAD.

I roll my eyes and sigh. I'm not interested in boring news, or pictures of Dad opening a new store or school in Shark Point. Dad loved to show off *before* he became mayor, but he's double worse now.

Dad pushes the octopiPAD right up close, and sensing that I'm not really

11

interested, he leans right in. "It's something even more interesting than knocking your own teeth out to win a silly prize. Look!"

I focus on the screen. It's not the boring news headline that I'm expecting. It's something way better:

NEW THIS SUMMER AT DREGOLAND!!!

SHARK POINT'S PREMIER AMUSEMENT PARK PRESENTS:

THE *MOST* TERRIFYING!

DORSAL-DEFYING!

SCARE-FEST IN
THE WHOLE WIDE OCEAN!!!

DARE YOU RIDE *THE KRAKEN???!!!!*

Dad fins the screen and a video plays . . . if my eyes bulged out when mom hugged me, then right now it must look like my whole face is about to explode!!!! And here's why:

Rising from the center of *Dregoland* are thirty *Gigantic! Green! Slimy! Tentacles!*

On each of the *tentacles* are about *twenty suckers!*

But as the video comes in closer, I can see the *suckers* are *cages!*

the KRAKEN

And in each cage is a kid shark or teen fish screaming with *joy* and *fear*!

But . . . the *tentacles* are whirling around the body of an *even GIGANTIC-ER mechanical kraken!!!!*

(Krakens are like the most feared *sea monsters* ever!)

The kraken's body is all *lumps* and *bumps* around a huge slippery mouth full of *terrible teeth*!

The *tentacles* swoop down *toward the teeth*!

Each tooth is as big as a great white!!!!

Everyone *screams.*

Everyone *laughs.*

It's the most exciting thing *I have ever seen!!!*

"Dad! Can we go?" I start swimming crazily around Dad's head. My swish-ing tail makes his sea-cereal float off toward the living room. "Can we, Dad? Can we?"

"Calm down, Harry!" Dad grabs me and floats me firmly back to the table.

"But—"

"You're not going anywhere, my son. Not until you've cleaned up my breakfast and picked up all those teeth."

Oh, fish cakes! In my excitement, I've knocked my jar of teeth all over the floor again. *Humph!*

CHAPTER 2

"Harry, stop!" Ralph yelps from inside my mouth.

"And then the Kraken's tentacles swoop down and . . ."

"Ouch! You just bit my *rear*! Ouch! Stop!"

". . . you're in the sucker cage and

you can't fall out, but it goes *right inside the kraken's mouth, upside down!*"

"Harry! How can I clean your teeth if—*ouch!*—you don't stop—*ouch!*—biting me? Just shut up about the stupid kraken, will you?"

Ralph darts out of my mouth and skids around to face me. He looks very angry. Ralph is my best friend. He's also a pilot fish, and pilot fish eat the bits of old food from between sharks' teeth. They're like swimming toothbrushes. Yeah, I know it sounds gross, but they seem to enjoy it. Well, mostly. I suppose it's not very enjoyable if the shark's mouth they're inside keeps talking about The Kraken and nipping them with the teeth they're supposed to be cleaning. But I'm so excited I just can't stop!

Ralph reaches a fin behind him and with a pained expression and a loud *pop* pulls one of my teeth out of his tender hide and slaps it into my fin.

"One more for your collection," Ralph says.

I put the tooth into my schoolbag. "Sorry, Ralph."

"You going to shut up now?" Ralph asks.

I nod and he swims back inside my mouth.

But all I can think about is The Kraken and riding in one of those cages on the craziest, mind-blowingest, amazingest theme park ride in the entire seaverse!

"What's up with Rick?" I ask my friend Joe the Jellyfish as we approach the school gates. Although I'm still totally stoked about The Kraken, I have to keep one side of my hammer on the lookout for trouble.

Rick's the school show off and can be a bit of a bully. He loves nothing more than sneaking up behind me and *flubbering* my hammer with his tail, then giggling with his dimwit buddy Donny Dogfish like a volcano's sea vent.

But Rick isn't lurking behind me today,

he's already by the gates strutting up and down in front of Cora and Pearl, the dolphin twins, and he's *smiling*.

Rick never smiles. Most times there's a sneer as wide as a walrus's bottom sliding up the side of his face.

"I don't like it," Joe says, "Rick's never that smiley."

To be fair, Joe doesn't like anything much. He's made of jelly in the bravery department as well as the body department. "He's up to something," Joe says quietly, and as if to make us all sure that he's scared by Rick's change of behavior, his bottom toots several times with fear.

Rick turns and struts again in front of the girls, pulling his mouth into a wider smile with his fins. As we get closer, my friend Tony the Tiger Shark nudges me in the gills with his finbow. "He's not smiling. Look."

I zero my hammer-vision in on Rick's mouth. Tony's right. He isn't smiling. He's showing off another couple of holes between his teeth to Cora and Pearl!

The dolphins flick their tails in excitement. "You're going to win for sure, Rick," coos Cora.

"You've lost more teeth than everyone else put together," purrs Pearl.

"Keep your heads down boys," I whisper to Ralph, Tony, and Joe as we get closer. "With any luck he won't notice us."

We *nearly* make it past when Joe's bottom *triple-toots*, and Rick spins around. His fake smile turns into a sneer, as if someone just flicked a switch on his face.

"Hey, rubberhead!"

My heart sinks lower than a sand skate's belly and my shoulders automatically hunch up. Rick floats right up to me, and I expect him to *flubber* me—but he doesn't. He just fins my mouth wide and looks right in.

"Pathetic!" he says after a moment, opening his mouth wide. Rick points at his lower jaw. "Ook at issssss!" Which, roughly translated, means, "Look at this!"

Rick has fresh spaces and I can see a few loose teeth. I think about pointing out my own new holes to Rick, but before I can raise a fin, Donny, who has sneaked up behind me, *flubbbbbbbbbbbbbbbbers* my hammer, and suddenly, Rick, Donny, Cora, and Pearl are all laughing their tail fins off.

Great.

"Harry Hammer?"

"Here . . . Ouch! . . . Mrs. Shelby."

Attendance isn't going well. Rick is sitting behind me in class flicking krill balls at the back of my hammer. Because Mrs. Shelby, our sea-turtle-teacher, is looking at her attendance book, she can't see what he's doing. She looks up. "Harry? What happened?"

I hear Rick growling under his breath. It's clear there will be trouble if I tell on him.

"Nothing, Mrs. Shelby. I just hit my finbow on the edge of the desk."

Mrs. Shelby continues with the attendance. Luckily Rick is too busy showing off his fresh holes to the kids around him to flick any more krill balls at me.

Some days I really don't want to be at school. Some days I wish I could be out in the ocean having adventures and ambushing prey just like my great white hero Gregor the Gnasher. No one would dare flick krill balls at him.

"Okay," Mrs. Shelby says. "As you all know it's only a week until we find out which shark has lost the most teeth this year, so let's have a count up!"

All the sharks in the class get their jars out and start counting. Only sharks are able to enter the competition because fish have really bad teeth that are so small you can barely see them, let alone count them. I tip my jar onto my desk. Ralph and Joe float over to help. Joe, being a jellyfish, comes in really handy—or really tentacle-y—because he can count things way quicker than anyone else. As all eight of his tentacles whirl around on my desk, my jar starts to fill up. I finish first.

"Two hundred and ninety-one!" I call out. Mrs. Shelby notes it down.

"Two hundred and seven, Mrs. Shelby,"

says Terry the Thresher Shark with a disappointed frown on his face. I'm *well* in the lead there!

"Two hundred and sixty-eight," Tony the Tiger Shark says. He smiles at me and gives me the fins-up.

"Two hundred and eighty," Lucy Lemon Shark calls out from the back of the class. I'm doing great!

Finally, there's only Rick left to call out his total and I'm still in the lead. Rick and Donny are counting. Their faces are deep in concentration. Rick may be good at sports, but he's not the sharpest tooth in the tooth jar when it comes to brainy

stuff, and they've had to restart a couple of times. Donny's become a bit cross-eyed with the pain of thinking, and his tongue is hanging out of his mouth. Mrs. Shelby goes over to their desk to help them.

Finally Rick looks up. "Two hundred and ninety-two!" he says triumphantly, and does three barrel rolls to celebrate.

Clams!

Ralph pokes me in the gills with his finbow.

I push his fin away.

Rick's in the lead—I really thought I might have a chance!

Ralph pokes me again.

"Get off!" I hiss at him.

Oh well. It's only a stupid old fake shark tooth for a prize. Not like it matters.

"Well," says Mrs. Shelby, "I have a very important and exciting announcement to make about this year's prize. I'm sure you've all seen the news about the new ride at Dregoland?"

Oh no. I don't like the sound of this.

Ralph is poking me so hard it's like he's trying to poke a hole through my gills. I push him away with my tail.

"I take great pleasure in informing you," Mrs. Shelby says, "that the owners of Dregoland have invited next week's winner, and three of his or her friends, to an exclusive preview night to be the first ever to ride The Kraken!"

I don't believe it!!!!!

"And," Mrs. Shelby continues, "the winner will get to meet the special guest of honor at the preview night—Gregor the Gnasher!"

I DOUBLE DON'T BELIEVE IT!!!!! Rick could get to ride The Kraken *and* meet my hero.

This is now officially the worst day of my life.

The whole class goes wild. Cora and Pearl rush up to Rick to pat him on the back and coo and purr at him all over again because he's in the lead. Donny and Rick are high-finning like crazy.

Ralph grabs me by the gills and shakes me hard. My head goes all *flubbery* and suddenly there's about ten Ralphs in front of me, all saying the same thing.

"Will you please take a look at my rear!"

"What?"

Ralph turns around and shoves his bottom in my face. "Look! I just found them and I can't reach them with my fins."

As my vision returns to normal I see two of my teeth still stuck in his hide.

Two teeth!

That means . . .

I pluck them out and hold them up high. "Mrs. Shelby! Look!"

Mrs. Shelby turns and looks in my fin.

"I have a new total! Two hundred and ninety-three!" I almost scream.

Everyone stops and stares. Cora and Pearl freeze in mid coo and look at me, my jar, and my two new teeth, freshly pulled from Ralph's rear.

"Well, that certainly puts you in the lead, Harry!" Mrs. Shelby smiles, and writes my new total down.

Suddenly everyone zooms away from

Rick and Donny like they're a bad smell and starts yelling and cheering and swimming around me!

I'm caught up in a whirlpool of noise and fins and jelly tentacles and tiger stripes.

Pearl and Cora lift me up on their bottlenoses and coo and purr thirty times louder than they did for Rick!

Rick and Donny don't join in of course. They've both floated to the back of the class with scowls so sharp they could pop a puffer fish.

Another great result!

This isn't such a bad day after all.

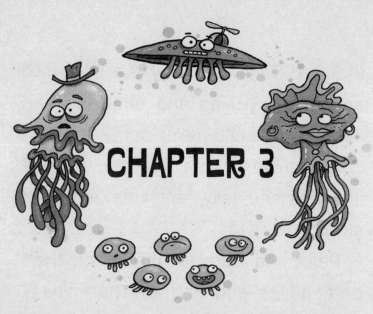

CHAPTER 3

"Yaaaaaaaaaaaaaaaaaaaaaaaaaaaaaaaaaaay!!!"

I bounce onto my bed and take the jar of teeth out of my schoolbag. Making sure that Humphrey and Larry aren't around, I give the jar a big sloppy kiss and place it carefully on my bedside crabinet.

I flop back onto my bed with a huge silly grin on my face and close my eyes. I imagine I'm in a cage on one of the Kraken legs, spinning through the water at a zillion krillometers an hour. Down below I can see hundreds and hundreds of faces—including Gregor the Gnasher's—cheering me on . . . and . . .

Rick's face suddenly looms up, filling my vision. He opens his mouth . . . and he has absolutely *no teeth at all*, and he's pointing at my mouth, which I can feel with my mouth is *full of teeth*! Then Mrs. Shelby is taking me by the fin and pulling me out of The Kraken and making me sit on the naughty rock for lying about my teeth. And now all I can see is Rick . . . with Gregor the Gnasher in the cage instead! He's flying above Dregoland. And he's laughing. And he's pointing. *At me!!!!!!!!!*

That's when I wake up.

What the heck! I must have drifted off to sleep and into a dream. Or more like a nightmare! I get a horrible scaredy feeling in the pit of my stomach as I realize I'm only one tooth ahead of Rick.

Just one.

He could easily overtake me in the next week.

I have to do something about it.

But what?

Time for a list. Lists always help. I get a pen and paper out of my bag. . . .

HOW TO MAKE MORE OF MY TEETH
FALL OUT THAN RICK

1. Go to Shark Park.

   Ummmm . . . then what?

2. Go to Shark Park and climb the jungle gym
   using only my *teeth!*

   *Bit ouchy. But . . . okay . . . no pain, no gain.
   What else?*

3. Dad's putting up shelves in the garage on the
   weekend.

   So . . . ?

4. I could offer to pass the shelves to him using
   only my *teeth!*

   *But that's not until the weekend and it might
   be too late by then. Think, Harry, think!*

5. I could turbo chomp my food all the time. That might loosen a few!

6. Distract Mom while she's cooking my trench toast in the morning so she burns it and makes it extracrunchy!

7. Pretend I'm pouring milk on my bowl of Kelp Krispies and eat them dry. That's bound to loosen a few. Those things are *evil* without milk!

8. Offer to open the cans of marine-beans for Mom, and when she's not looking, use my teeth.

9. Dad has a whole box of supercrunchy toffees in his office left over from Christmas. I'll sneak into Dad's office, get the toffees, and loosen a dozen teeth with them, easy!

I look back at the list. Surely, if I do all of them, I will beat Rick.

"Harry-Warry," I hear Mom calling up the stairs, "It's time to come down for dinner!"

"Okay, Mom," I shout, darting off my bed and head for the door. Time to lose a few more teeth.

I wonder what hard and crunchy food Mom has cooked for me tonight? *Lobster still in its shell*? Yes, I can loosen my teeth on that. I head down the hallway. Or maybe it's *mussels in coral gravy*? Bunches of shells there for me to get my teeth into. I zoom down the stairs. Or *whale steak*, well done, with a lovely fat bone for me

44

to crunch my teeth on. Yes! Losing those extra teeth and winning a ride on The Kraken is going to be a piece of *fish*cake!

I skid into the kitchen, where Mom is dishing up food, and Dad is flicking through his octopiPAD.

"Mom! Mom! What's for dinner?" I ask excitedly. I can't wait to sink my teeth into it.

Mom puts a big steaming bowl onto the table in front of me. "There you go, Harry. Sea-cucumber soup to start, followed by soft-crab-egg salad, and lovely sea-strawberry pudding for dessert. Eat up."

Whaaaaaaaaaaat??????????????

My heart sinks so fast I think it might plop right out of my bottom!

I have to think quickly. There's no way I can just have soup, soft eggs, and pudding—they won't help my teeth fall out at all. I look around the kitchen, desperately trying to find something to add to the soup to toughen it up. . . .

Yes!

I see a big bag of nuts on the table next to Dad. They're not his usual brand, but I don't care. The bag is too close to Dad for me to get them without him seeing, and there's no way he's going to

46

give me his favorite after-dinner snack.

I desperately try to think up a plan.

Okay. This might work. . . .

I swim up from the table, knowing Mom will tell me to go back and eat my soup.

"Harry, get back to the table!" she says.

Perfect.

"But, Mom, I thought I heard someone at the door. It might be important. I should go and see."

"No, eat your soup. Hugo, will you go and see who's at the door please?"

Dad sighs as he puts down the Octo-piPAD. "But I haven't read everything they've written about me yet!"

Mom gives him one of her hardest stares.

Dad gets up from the table and heads for the door.

"Mom, can you smell something burning?" I ask innocently as I move toward the bag of nuts on the table.

Mom looks around wildly. "Burning? Where?"

"Dunno, Mom, maybe the oven?" I keep my eyes firmly fixed on Mom as I feel along the table with my tail and flick the bag of nuts toward my bowl of soup. Mom looks all around the oven with her hammer-vision to check to see if anything is wrong.

I quickly tip the bag of nuts into my soup bowl.

Mission accomplished!

I hide the empty bag under the table as Dad comes back in.

"No one there," he huffs. "Must be those silly kid-squids playing practical jokes again. I'll have to speak to their parents!"

I take a huge spoonful of soup and move it toward my mouth.

"Hang on," says Dad, "Where has my bag of nuts gone?"

I put the spoon in my mouth and prepare to take the hardest *chomp* I can.

"I need those nuts for the weekend," Dad says. "I got them to go on the bolts to hold the shelves together. They're special ones covered in whale-stomach oil so they go on really easy."

I freeze, mid-*chomp*.

Whale stomach oil?!

The first horrible tang of flavor reaches the back of my mouth and I start feeling really sick.

Unable to stop myself, I spit the soup and nuts across the table and watch as they *bounce* and *ping* off Mom and Dad's hammers.

This is going to take some explaining.

Once I've cleaned up all the soup and whale-stomach-oil nuts, eaten another bowl of soup, then the soft-crab-egg salad, and the even softer custard, all the time being watched like a seahawk by my parents, I'm allowed to go back to my bedroom.

I float at my desk, still feeling a little

icky and turn on my laptop—at least chatting with my pals on Plaicebook might cheer me up.

Wrong!

How about double-wrong with a double helping of triple-wrong with nineteen kinds of special-wrong all on top?

The first thing that comes up in my feed is a huge picture of Rick. His holey smile is back and he's holding a freshly removed tooth in his fin.

The caption underneath makes me feel even sicker. I'M GONNA HAMMER HARRY!!!!

The picture has seventy-four likes.

I slam the laptop closed and begin a seriously fin-folded, face-screwed-up, dorsal-trembling huff!

I run my tongue across the rows of teeth in my mouth really hoping I can find more loose ones. But other than the one that's already a tiny bit wobbly I can't find any!

I'm beginning to think it would have been better if I'd chomped down on every whale-stomach-oil nut in my soup and broken every tooth in my head!

What am I going to do???

CHAPTER 4

"What the heck," says Ralph, swimming out of my mouth the next morning as him, Joe, Tony, and me make our way to school. "You're more miserable than a clown fish who's been fired from the sea-circus!"

Ralph's right. I hardly slept last night thinking about Rick.

Tony and Joe start a quick game of finball as we reach school, but I tell them I don't want to play. "I just don't feel like it," I say as Rick and Donny come strutting in.

"Hey, rubberhead, check this out!" says Rick, holding up his Seaberry smartphone. His picture on Plaicebook has more than a hundred and fifty likes. That's nearly every kid and squid in school! "Looks like I'm gonna *hammer* you, Harry!"

Donny, Cora, and Pearl laugh like a whale rear end with an upset tummy. Rick waves his Seaberry around to anyone who wants to look.

"Harry! Watch out!" I hear Joe shout behind me. Tony's finball thuds into my dorsal with a stinging thwack!

"Sorry," Tony says, "I finned it too hard—" But I don't get to hear the rest of his apology because the force of the

finball pushes me through the water straight into Rick!

Rick bounces off me and nosedives into Cora's schoolbag, which is open near her tail.

Rick's Seaberry spins off into the

current and over the school's coral wall.

Rick, yelling and twisting, finally gets his head out of Cora's bag. He has three of her sparkling pink necklaces wrapped around his nose, a wonky line of pink lipstick around his mouth, and three of her fake blond hair extensions floating up from his ears.

There's a moment of terrible silence.

Then everyone in the playpool starts to laugh!

I get ready for Rick

to come over and flubber me—or worse—
but Donny points to the wall where Rick's
Seaberry disappeared, and they both swim
off to find it. I can see from the way Rick's
shaking his fins that he is *very* angry.

He's not going to let this go.

As soon as we're in the swimnasium for
PE, I can see that Rick is planning something. Mrs. Shelby has split us into teams
for finball, and Rick and Donny are on
the other side. I spend the first couple of
minutes just trying to stay out of Rick's
way, instead of trying to get the ball.

"Come on, Harry!" calls Mrs. Shelby from the sidelines. "It's finball, not water ballet!"

Rick brushes past me and I feel his finbow crunch into my side. "No one makes an idiot of me," he hisses as he goes past.

Ralph gets the ball at the halfway line and dribbles brilliantly around Donny. Going forward, he fins the ball to Tony, who sidefloats around Cora and fins the ball in a great spinning loop up over Rick (who's zooming toward him) straight to me!

Well, I have no choice now. I zip

forward, fin left, fin right—zoom beneath Pearl and head toward the goal . . .

Crash!!!

Suddenly I'm spinning up to the roof of the swimnasium and bouncing head-first into the ceiling.

Sparkly starfish explode near my head and spin around me crazily.

I tumble upside down in a couple of lazy spins and thud into

the floor. I can dimly hear Mrs. Shelby telling Rick off for his "Terrible tackle on Harry!" as Joe, Ralph, and Tony rush over to me to help.

"Are you all right, Harry?" Ralph calls.

"Harry, buddy, that looked bad," says Tony, rubbing my hammer where it crunched into the ceiling.

Joe's bottom toots several times, but I know that's because he's worried.

Normally I'd be really angry, but this time I think it's super.

A big smile spreads across my face.

"Oh no!" cries Ralph, "Harry's delirious! Call a clambulance!"

I hold up my fin. "No, it's okay! Look!"
I stick out my tongue.

They all stare at the tooth lying on it.
It was knocked out when my head hit
the ceiling.

"I'm back in the lead!" I yell, spinning back up with a howl of triumph.

Rick looks totally shocked. He zooms away from Mrs. Shelby, heading straight for me!

I don't want a fight, but it looks like I might have no choice.

Rick wrenches my mouth open with his fins. Then he grabs the tooth from me and starts trying to shove it back into my gum. "It's not fair, it's not fair, *it's not fair!*" he yells.

Mrs. Shelby has to pull Rick off me and give him a good talking to about fair play and rough tackles and

not sticking my teeth back in without
permission.

At lunch break everyone's talking about
what happened in the swimnasium and
I'm back to being Mr. Popular again. Rick
and Donny are scowling at me from
across the playpool.

Ralph is picking bits of lunch out from
between my teeth. "Not a bad job, even
if I do say so myself," he says proudly
as he swims out of my mouth. "You have
the cleanest teeth in the school."

I nod and feel around with my tongue

to see if there are any fresh wobblers, but sadly all my teeth feel very sturdy and strong.

Rick and Donny are whispering to each other. Rick looks agitated and Donny keeps pointing in my direction.

"What are they up to?" I say to my friends.

"Dunno, Harry, but I reckon you're safe from attack after what happened this morning," Ralph replies. "Rick won't want to risk knocking out any more of your teeth."

But Ralph may have spoken too soon because Rick is now zooming across the playpool straight at me! His face is angry, his mouth is sneery, and his tail is swishing powerful strokes, speeding him up and up and up.

Ralph tries to pull me out of the way, but I'm not sure which direction to go. Rick could still change course. The other kids all get out of his way and their faces turn toward me to watch the upcoming battle.

But . . .

Rick goes right past me!

But?

What?

Clannnnnnnnnnnnnnnnnnnnnnnnnnnnnnn-nngggggggg!!!!

I turn just in time to see Rick crash at full speed into the playpools jungle gym.

Clannnnnnnnnnnnnnnnnnnnnngggggggg!!!!

Rick bounces off one prong and *boings* into another.

As he comes to a stop, cross-eyed and nose-bent, I can see he's smiling in the same way I did in the swimnasium, except this time . . .

Spit.

One!

Spit.

Two!!

Spit.

Three!!!

Spit.

Four!!!!

Spit.

FIVE!!!!!

. . . freshly broken teeth come out of Rick's mouth. All around the playpool kids start cheering.

For Rick!

"Harry, stop! Don't be an idiot!" Ralph is pulling at my fin, but I'm determined. I'm not going to stop. "Harry you can't do this. You can't!"

It's after school and I'm dragging Ralph down the street because he's stuck to my fin like a stubborn barnacle and I'm heading for the nearest shop that has what I need.

Ralph is pulling at me, but I'm too strong. "I can't let you do this, Harry. As your friend and floating toothbrush I can't let you do this to yourself."

"I have no choice!" I shout at him. "Rick's four in the lead now! Four! How am I going to catch up if I don't do something drastic?"

"I don't know, but this isn't the answer."

We stop outside the sweet shop. I pull Ralph off my fin and reach in to my schoolbag for my money. "Now you stay there; I don't need you whining in my ear."

"No, Harry. No!" Ralph frowns at me. "If you go in there and buy all that candy in the hope that it will rot out more of your teeth, then I resign as your toothbrush!"

"No need!" I yell.

"Why?" Ralph says hopefully. "Have you changed your mind?"

"No. There's no need to resign because you're fired!"

And with that, I storm into the shop, leaving Ralph outside with the *shockingest* shocked look of all time on his face.

CHAPTER 5

This is me: "Owwwwwwwwwwww-
wwwwwwwwwwwwwwwwwwwwww-
wwwwwwwwwwwwwwwwwwwwww-
wwwwwwwwwwwwwwwwwwwwww-
wwwwwwwwwwwwwwwwwwwww-
wwwwwwwwwwwwwwwwwwww-
wwwwwwww!!!!!!!!"

This is Mom: "What's the matter?!"

This is me: "Owwwwwwwwwwwwwwww-
wwwwwwwwwwwwww-
wwwwwwwwwwwwww-
wwwwwwwwwwwwwww-
wwwwwwwwwwwwwww-
wwwwwwwwwwwwwwwwwwwww-
wwwwwwwwwwwwwwwwwwwwww-
wwwwwwwwwwww!!!!!!!!"

This is Mom: "Tell me, Harry! Should I call a clambulance? Hugo! Hugo!"

This is me: "Owwwwwwwwwwww-
wwwwwwwwwwwwwwwwwwwwwww-

74

wwwwwwwwwwwwwwwwwww-
wwwwwwwwwwwwwwwwwwww-
wwwwwwwwwwwwwwwwwwwww-
wwwwwwwwwwwwwwwwwwwww-
wwwwwwwww!!!!!!!!"

This is Mom: "Hang on . . . what are all those candy wrappers doing under your bed? Coral Crunchies? Krillix? Fishstar Bars? Sherbet Bluetip? Have you been eating all this candy, Harry? Have you given yourself a toothache?"

This is me: "Owwwwwwwwwww-
wwwwwwwwwwwwwwwwwwww-
wwwwwwwwwwwwwwwwwwww-
wwwwwwwwwwwwwwwwwwww-

wwwwwwwwwwwwwwwwwwww-
wwwwwwwwwwwwwwwwwwwww-
wwwwwwwww!!!!!!!!"

This is Mom: "Hugo! Call the dentist!"
This is me: "Noooooooooo! Owww-
wwww! Noooooooooo! Owwwwwww!
Noooooooooo! Owwwwwww! Noooooooooo!

Owwwwwww! Noooooooooo! Owwwwwww! Noooooooooo! Owwwwwww!"

This is Humphrey and Larry:
"Hahahahahahahahahahahahahaha-
hahahahahahahahahahahahahahaha-
hahahahahahahaha!!!"

And this is me in the dentist's waiting
room feeling very sorry for myself.

It's Saturday morning and I've been
dragged to the dentist instead of out playing with my friends. I've been dragged
to the dentist because for the last four
days I've been spending every penny

of my allowance on candy in the hope that it will rot my teeth and make them fall out faster. So I've been dragged to the dentist because I've given myself a *massive* toothache.

And do you know what?

Yup.

That's right.

Not one single extra tooth has fallen out! All I'm left with is the worst toothache anyone in the history of the seaverse has ever had. You leggy air breathers might think it's terrible having one toothache. Try having *eighteen*!

Mom is usually all "mushy" with me when I'm sick, but I can tell this time she is superangry.

"It's your own fault!" she says as she flicks through the magazines from the waiting room table. "As a shark, you know that looking after your teeth is really important. Especially because you have so many."

I don't argue with her because I know she's right—and also because opening my mouth is agony. I just nod and feel extra sorry for myself. And more than a little bit scared. And more than a lot bit in pain. It feels like Ralph is in my mouth nailing tiny pictures to my teeth.

Ow.

Then I hear a noise that makes me freeze with fear.

Zzzzzzzz—ket ket ket—zzzzzzzz—ket ket ket.

The noise is coming from the exam room, floating into the waiting room through the dentist's door.

It makes my tummy turn into seaweed-spaghetti knots. I look up at Mom for some comfort. But she just makes that mom-face at me. You know, the face that moms always make when they're using their eyes to tell you what a goofball you've been.

I try closing my eyes.

But that just makes me imagine what could be happening to make that

81

*zzzzzzzz—ket ket ket—zzzzzzzz—
ket ket ket* noise, which won't stop, and
keeps getting louder . . . and . . .

*ZZZZZZZ—KET KET KET—ZZZZZZZ—
KET KET KET.*

. . . louder.

"Mom, Mom, there's been a miracle,"
I say, grabbing her fin. "My toothache
is completely gone. Quick, let's go
home."

Mom reaches into her bag and pulls
out a sea apple and plops it into my
fin. "If your toothache is gone, then
why don't you eat this nice crunchy sea
apple?"

I look at the crunchy sea apple.

I look at Mom.

There's no way I can eat it.

Mom does the mom-face and takes the sea apple back.

"Harry Hammer?"

I look up. The dentist's door is open and the eight-tentacled, orange-skinned, ink-expelling dentist, Doctorpus Jones is looking right at me with her huge

eyes. "Would you like to come in?" she says.

"Oh." I say quickly, "I didn't realize I had a choice. In that case, no. I wouldn't."

But before I can make my escape, Mom fins me in the back and sends me floating straight into the wriggly tentacles of the dentist. The dentist does something strange with her mouth. I think it's supposed to be a smile, but it just makes me think of chopped squid strips in gravy.

I want to turn away from Doctorpus Jones and all of her tentacles, but Mom is right behind me, and soon we're in the dimly lit exam room. I look around wildly for whatever machine was making that *zzzzzzzz—ket ket ket—zzzzzzzz—ket ket ket* noise.

Doctorpus Jones leads me to a chair with two of her tentacles, while shaking Mom by the fin with another, while tinkling in a tray of instruments with three more, while holding up my paperwork to her eyes with another, while scratching an itch on her head with the last one.

It's very confusing describing an octopus multitask.

Doctorpus Jones settles me in the chair with two tentacles, while putting

85

on her mask with two others, while pulling up her chair with three more, and pushing her glasses up her nose with the last. I start to worry about what's coming next. I still haven't worked out what made that horrible noise, and I'm getting very nervous about it.

"Let's have a look shall we?" says Doctorpus Jones, pulling at my chin with two tentacles, while holding up some silvery dentist tools with four others.

The dim light in the exam room glints off the shiny tools and flickers across the room. It's like being trapped in the world's scariest disco.

Mom holds my fin. I'm not sure if it's to comfort me or stop me from swimming away at top speed!

Zzzzzzzz—ket ket ket—zzzzzzzz—ket ket ket.

Terrified, I leap from the chair, dragging Mom with me, and crash into the ceiling.

"What's that noise?" I yell in terror. "What are you going to do to me?"

Doctorpus Jones has to use seven tentacles to grab hold of me and one to anchor herself to the chair. "Oh, that," she says with another of her weird smiles. "That's my coffee machine. I can't get through a morning's *dentisting* without my coffee!"

She points one of her tentacles to a coffee machine hiding in the shadows at the back of the exam room.

Zzzzzzzz—ket ket ket—zzzzzzzz—ket ket ket.

Zzzzzzzz—ket ket ket—zzzzzzzz—ket ket ket.

"Coffee's ready!" says Doctorpus Jones.

I feel *very* stupid.

Back in the chair again, Doctorpus Jones gets down to

business, holding my chin with two tentacles, while exploring my mouth with three tentacles, while writing her notes with two others, while stirring her fresh cup of coffee with the last.

"Well, Harry," she says, "What a silly

boy you've been. Just to win a competition you've given yourself a horrible toothache, and I'm going to have to give you eighteen fillings."

I feel *very* sorry for myself.

"But don't worry, the fillings will make those teeth a lot stronger, so they'll last much longer."

"So they won't fall out before Monday?" I ask.

"No, Harry. They'll probably still be there next year."

Great.

"And before we begin, I see from your paperwork that you've fired your pilot fish." Doctorpus Jones frowns at me. "Let me tell you, Harry, there's nothing more important to your teeth than a good pilot fish giving them a clean twice a day. I don't ever want to see you here without a pilot fish again. Is that clear?"

I nod sadly.

"Good, then we'll begin."

Eighteen fillings later, we're leaving the exam room and my mouth feels like someone has stuffed two finballs in it. At least the pain's gone, but my

lips are so numb, I can't speak without dribbling.

Mom's being more sympathetic now as she holds my fin, taking great care not to squeeze it too much.

"Hello, rubberhead!" a voice hisses in my ear. I look up. It's Rick!

Just what I need right now—Rick seeing me like this.

Rick's with his mom, Rosy Reef. While his mom and my mom chat about boring stuff, Rick stares at me with a huge holey smile. "What's up with your mouth, rubberhead?"

"Ish been to tsh dentisht."

"Say it, don't spray it!" Rick laughs.

"Ish hash had an anaeshtheshtic."

"Are you saying I've been ship-wrecked?" Rick smirks.

"Nosh! Ish hash had an an-aesh-thesh-tic!"

"Are you saying you've become a spit monster?"

"Nosh!"

"Can't wait to tell everyone at school you've turned into a spit monster!" Rick says gleefully.

Great.

The worst Saturday ever just got even worse.

Later that afternoon there's a knock on my bedroom door. Still feeling really sorry for myself, I go to open it.

It's Ralph.

"I got your text," he mutters.

Ralph still looks pretty angry, but at least he came.

My mouth has been reduced to just one finball size now, and my lips are working properly again.

Mostly.

"What do you want?" Ralph asks suspiciously.

"I wanted to apologishe."

"Yeah, I bet you do. But only because you want me back so you don't have to see Doctorpus Jones again."

I shake my hammer. "No—I've been silly. You're my besht friend, and I'd have you back even if you didn't clean my teesh again."

"Really?"

"Yesh. Really."

Ralph looks relieved. "I've missed you too. I will come back, and I will continue cleaning your teeth. Okay?"

"Thanksh."

Ralph looks at my bedside crabinet and sees that I've been writing. "What's that?"

"A lisht."

"A *lisht*?" Ralph grins.

"Don't you shtart. I had enough of that from Rishk outshide the dent-isht."

"What is it a list of?"

I show him.

LIST OF HOW TERRIBLE
MY LIFE IS RIGHT NOW

1. Ralph is not my friend.

2. I have a mouth full of filled teeth.

3. I have a mouth full of filled teeth that will
   probably *never* fall out.

4. Rick is going to make my life a misery at
   school because of it.

5. I will definitely not win the competition now.

6. I won't get to ride The Kraken.

7. I won't get to meet Gregor the Gnasher.

8. And Rick will!

"Well, you can cross off number one
for a start," says Ralph.

With my best attempt at a smile, I cross off number one.

But Rick is still going to win the competition, and he's still going to ride The Kraken, and he's still going to get to meet Gregor, and I'm still going to be the dorky rubberheaded shark who everyone laughs at.

This is probably the worst day of my life.

I flop down onto my bed and put my hammer in my fins.

Even with Ralph back, my life is a disaster.

CHAPTER 6

"How many fell out over the weekend?" asks Tony.

I sigh.

It's Monday, the day the competition ends, and Joe, me, Ralph, and Tony are heading to school as usual. Apart from the fact that I still can't eat anything crunchy or hard, my mouth is pretty much back to normal. I shake my hammer sadly. "None. Not a single one. Doctorpus Jones's fillings have stuck them in like rock. Rick's gonna win for sure."

The rest of the term is going to be quintuple-awful with Rick gloating about winning. He's a show off at the best of times, but winning a ride on The Kraken is going to turn him into a nightmare.

Cora and Pearl are waiting at the school gates.

"Where's Rick?" Cora calls as Donny swims up alone.

Donny shrugs. "Dunno. Haven't heard from him since Saturday."

Probably wants to make an entrance because he knows he's won, I think bitterly.

A taxicrab screeches to a halt outside the school gates, and Rick's mom, Rosy, gets out. "Come on Rick, don't worry, no one's going to laugh at you. Get out."

What???

I float closer, wondering what's going on. A crowd of kids gather around the taxicrab and we watch as Rick fins his way out and proves his mom totally wrong.

Everyone laughs.

Even the taxicrab is chuckling to himself.

When I bumped into Rick on Saturday I didn't realize that he was on his way to Dotorpus Jones too! He must have really damaged his mouth slamming into the clamming frame at school, because his mouth has been wired up with an enormous steel brace. The metal climbs out of his mouth, goes up the side of his face, and ends in a huge wing nut on top of his head.

He looks like an accident in a gate factory!

Laughter follows Rick as his mom grabs his fin and steers him through the school gates. As they pass by Rick glares at me. "Shhhhsssht issssssth usssssssth wasssssssssssssssht!!!!"

"Sorry?" I say, with a huge filling-filled grin, "Did you say you've just come from a fancy dress party dressed as a gate?"

"Sshsh! Krssssssssssssht!"

"Say it, don't spray it!"

Although I know he's still going to win the competition, I do feel a little bit better.

In class everyone is really excited about the result.

Except me.

Instead of counting out our jars ourselves, we have to hand them in to Mrs. Shelby, and she will count them out for us.

Rick tails my desk as he makes his way past, but I manage to stop my jar from falling over.

Talk about a sore loser, Rick's even a sore winner!

Ralph's eyes are bulging out looking

at all the teeth in all the jars lined up on Mrs. Shelby's desk. I can tell he's thinking of the food that might be left on them and I can hear his tummy rumbling. I pass him the last uneaten krispies bar from my bag and he gobbles it up quickly with a smile.

I take my jar up to Mrs. Shelby so that she can start counting. On her desk I see the Drego-land ticket for the exclusive preview of The Kraken.

Great.

So close and yet so far.

I look around, and see Gate-Face-Rick at the back of the class with Donny. They're looking at the new Dregoland brochure, which has an awesome picture of The Kraken on the front. Rick is pointing at it and Donny is nodding happily.

I return to my desk in a huff.

"Don't worry, buddy," says Tony, seeing how upset I am. "You can go with your parents another time. It's not the end of the world."

No, it's not.

It's *worse* than the end of the world.

I shrug at Tony, "It's all right for you;

you don't care about winning. But Rick beats me at everything, and there's nothing he likes more than rubbing my hammer in it. He's going to be showing off about this for months."

Tony turns away with a smile. "It really won't be the end of the world if you don't beat Rick, you know."

When she finally finishes counting, Mrs. Shelby floats up in front of her desk. "Well, it's been an excellent competition this year, and it's been very close!"

Everyone except me cheers.

I sink right down in my seat.

"For quite some time, Rick and Harry

have been hammer and nose, and we've all been excited as their totals went up," Mrs. Shelby continues, fixing me and Rick with a hard stare. "I can't say I approve of their methods during the last few weeks, but at least now they've both ended up at the dentist, and they've learned how important it is to treat their teeth with respect."

I'm sinking so low in my chair I'm in danger of sliding under my desk. I fold my fins across my chest.

Just get it over with.

"And that's why I'm glad to announce that the winner is . . ."

I can hear Rick starting to get up from his desk. . . .

"Is . . ."

Oh, get it over with!

". . . Tony the Tiger Shark!"

Everyone goes wild.

"What?" I yell.

"Wasssth?!" shouts Rick.

"Y e s s s s s s !" shouts Tony, doing twenty-four bar-rel rolls over-head. When he stops, he looks straight at me.

110

"See? I told you it wasn't the end of the world. My dad burned my dinner last night; it was so crunchy it knocked bunches and bunches of loose teeth out!"

I high-fin Tony seven times.

Gate-Face-Rick has flopped back into his chair, and Donny looks like he's been slapped in the face with a wet anchovy.

Score!

Mrs. Shelby hands Tony the Dregoland ticket and he holds it in his fins like it's the most precious thing in the world.

Because it is!

"Well done, Tony." Mrs. Shelby smiles.

"Now, who are you going to take with you to ride on The Kraken?"

The classroom is suddenly silent.

Cora flicks her hair and Pearl flutters her eyelashes at Tony. Joe's bottom toots with tension so many times he's propelled across the classroom like a rocket into the window. "Sorry," he says from his now inside-out face.

Tony looks around the class. "I'm going to take Joe the Jellyfish!"

Joe toots, zooms, and hits the wall with a splat.

POP! POP! POP!

"I'm also taking Ralph the Pilot Fish!"

Ralph does four somersaults and goes green and looks sick, but still has a crazy smile on his face.

"And lastly . . ."

The whole class stares at Tony. Pearl's eyelashes are setting a new world record for fluttering.

Tony looks straight at Rick.

No! No! No!

Rick's eyes light up. He can't believe it.

I can't believe it!

"And lastly . . . I'm taking . . ."

"Yesssssssth, yessssssht, yessssssht!" says Rick.

"I'm taking . . . *Harry Hammer!!!!!*"

No.

Yes.

No?

Yes!!

Hooray!!!!

I zoom above the class with Tony, Ralph, and Joe, high-finning, yelling, and screaming.

Not only am I going to see Gregor the Gnasher and ride on The Kraken with all my best friends and Rick isn't, but because he can't open his mouth to speak, he won't be able to call me rubberhead or any other names.

Finally, I have something to smile about—even if my mouth is full of fillings!

THE END

Meet Harry and the Shark Point gang. . . .

HARRY

Species:

hammerhead shark

You'll spot him . . .

using his special

hammer-vision

Favorite thing:

his Gregor the Gnasher

poster

Most likely to say:

"I wish I was a great white."

Most embarrassing moment: when Mom called him

her "little starfish" in front of all his friends

RALPH

Species:

pilot fish

You'll spot him . . .

eating the food from

between Harry's teeth!

Favorite thing: shrimp Pop-Tarts

Most likely to say: "So, Harry, what's for

breakfast today?"

Most embarrassing moment: eating too much cake

on Joe's birthday. His face was COVERED in pink

plankton icing.

JOE

Species: jellyfish

You'll spot him . . . hiding behind Ralph and Harry, or behind his own tentacles

Favorite thing: his cave, since it's nice and safe

Most likely to say: "If we do this, we're going to end up as fish food. . . ."

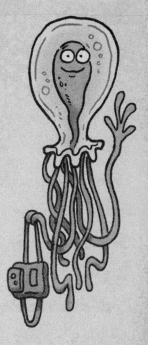

Most embarrassing moment: whenever his rear goes *toot*, which is when he's scared. Which is all the time.

RICK

Species: blacktip reef shark

You'll spot him . . .

bullying smaller fish

or showing off

Favorite thing: his black

leather jacket

Most likely to say:

"Last one there's a sea snail!"

Most embarrassing moment:

none. Rick's far too cool to get embarrassed.

Join Zeus and his friends as they set off on the adventure of a lifetime.

Now Available:

FOLLOW THE TRAIL AND SOLVE MYSTERIES WITH FRANK AND JOE!

HardyBoysSeries.com